THE CREEPY TALES FROM KENSINGTONVILLE

BEDTIME

Kenneth Spencer Jr

THE CREEPY TALES FROM KENSINGTONVILLE

BEDTIME

First printed in Great Britain by Kenneth Spencer Jr. 2007

ISBN-13: 978-09555973-0-5

www.kennethspencerjr.com

The Creepy Tales from Kensingtonville

Bedtime

For Kyle, Corey and Jemel

Introduction

Kensingtonville

In a place far, far away, so far away in fact, that you may not have heard of it until now, there was a small village by the name of Kensingtonville. The village was so small that everybody knew each other and at times there was never anything to do.

Like the way times used to be long ago in the world, the wives of Kensingtonville stayed at home and looked after the house whilst their husbands went off to work and their children went to school.

The village was a safe and quiet place for its residents to live in, they could walk about feeling safe and content, day or night, and everyone in the village was happy with the way their lives were.

The wives of Kensingtonville would often get together and talk about how they took care of their homes, because although their husbands went out to work and paid the bills and would often use the phrase 'This is my house and you will do as I say,' when telling their children off, it was their wives who cooked, cleaned and spent more time in the house. So really, in all fairness, even though it was the man's house, it was the woman's home. Because of this, the wives of Kensingtonville took pride in everything they did in and around the house. When one wife visited another they could spend hours on the same subject and never tire of it.

The wives of Kensingtonville didn't just visit each other and talk about their homes, cooking and cleaning, they did much more than that. As a family, they would take their children on trips to the seaside and they would play cricket, football and go to the movies with their husbands. They also had Committee meetings down at the Kensingtonville community hall every Wednesday evening at 6pm sharp while their husbands stayed in and looked after the children.

The wives of Kensingtonville couldn't have thought of a better place to live on God's green earth and would not want to, because to them Kensingtonville was the friendliest, safest and prettiest village of them all.

If the women enjoyed it greatly, the men did even more so. They woke up nice and early and after taking their time to eat the most scrumptious breakfast, that consisted of; bacon and eggs, two slices of toast and the loveliest cup of tea in the whole, wide world, which their wives took time and effort to prepare, they kissed their wives and children goodbye and left the house. Off to work they went, where they would spend a full eight hours, not a minute more or a minute less, before returning home to spend time with their families. However, work and family were not the only things the men of Kensingtonville thought of. Although to the men of Kensingtonville the most important thing above all was to care and provide for their families and nothing on God's green earth would ever come before it, the men had their fun too. Like their wives, they would play cricket, football and go to the movies with their children, but they also had their Committee meetings, Chess clubs, Bowls clubs and any other club you could think of forming in a small village like Kensingtonville. The husbands of Kensingtonville couldn't have thought of a better place to live on God's green earth and would not want to, because to them Kensingtonville was the friendliest, safest and prettiest village of them all.

For the children of Kensingtonville the weekdays were boring because they had to get up early and go to school. They had to be in bed by seven which most of them hated because they all liked to stay up late, even when they were barely still awake.

The younger children were especially notorious for being half asleep and still not wanting to go to bed. They would be sleeping in the armchair, in the living room and when their mother or father would notice and call to them to get up and go to bed, they would spring up like a jack in the box, their eyes would snap wide open and they would have sworn that they weren't asleep and just resting their eyes, or that they had to close them for just a second because the television was too bright and they needed to refocus them.

What the children of Kensingtonville hated most about weekdays was the fact that their school teachers would give them homework, as if six hours a day at school wasn't enough they wanted them to do more at home! Like children don't have anything better to do!

The weekends however, were what the children lived for. They stayed up until nine and some of the parents even let them stay up until nine-thirty if there was a film on T.V that they were watching and it hadn't finished yet. The younger children played all day and invented new games when they got bored of playing the old ones. The older children, went shopping, to the movies and hung out at the village diner with their friends. As for homework, after they had finished it on the Friday evening, which they did extraordinarily faster than usual, the children forgot the word "homework" was even in existence, until Monday came around again and their teachers announce they would be getting some more!.

Other than the early bedtimes and the truck loads of homework that the children got during the week, life was sweet for the children of Kensingtonville, and like their mothers and fathers there wasn't anywhere else on

God's green earth that the children would want to live because, to them, Kensingtonville was the friendliest, safest and prettiest village of them all.

Although there are many stories to tell of the people that lived in Kensingtonville the story that is about to be told only focuses on three boys; Corey, Jemel and most of all a boy named Kyle. By the way, the above statement I just made about Kensingtonville being the safest and happiest place of them all, to be honest with you, is not entirely true! I should have really said; Kensingtonville was the safest, friendliest, and prettiest village of them all for ninety-nine point nine percent of the people that lived in the small village. Kyle, felt exactly the same as everyone else about Kensingtonville being the happiest and safest place of all… well, at least that is, until Night Fall.

For Kyle, when the sun went down and the moon came up he got scared. In truth Kyle Mackenzie was the biggest scaredy cat who ever lived in Kensingtonville, although he wouldn't admit it. Other children were scared of things, his two best friends, Corey and Jemel were afraid of things and although they wouldn't let the younger kids know, the older children were afraid of things too. However Kyle was afraid of everything, he would jump at the slightest noise and he was even afraid of his own shadow at times but most of all for

Kyle Mackenzie of Kensingtonville bed time was the scariest time of all.

Chapter One

Daylight

Though Kyle was awake he dared not open his eyes, fearful of the horrid surprise that awaited him if it was night and the moon was still shining. Kyle laid under his covers with his eyes shut tightly waiting for the rap that he heard every morning, the light rap of his mother's or father's hand against the door which Kyle took as the sign that it was morning and safe to open his eyes and get out of bed.

Kyle loved his bed, and he loved to sleep, he just didn't like going to bed, or that moment between actually getting into bed and falling asleep, because like most eight year olds, Kyle was afraid of the dark, more afraid than any other kid in Kensingtonville, so very afraid that he would try his utmost to stay up for as long as possible with his mother and father where he felt safe. He would eat his dinner with rabbit bite mouthfuls, nibble on his nibbles and he would sit at the table for almost up to a whole hour after his parents had finished eating. This at times would make his parents very annoyed. "Kyle, if you don't like the food, then just leave it!" Mrs Mackenzie would say as she went back into the dining room and saw him still nibbling away.

"Mummy your food is so lovely that I want it to last forever and ever." Kyle would reply with a big grin on his face. The first two times Kyle said this to his mother she thought it was the biggest compliment she had ever received from her doting son, but when the response became routine, she began to wonder whether he really meant it or not. It's true Kyle loved his mother's cooking, but what he didn't tell her was that he ate slowly because it meant that it prolonged his bedtime so he could stay up longer. After his dinner he had to do his home work then he was allowed to go downstairs and watch television with his mother and father for another half an hour before he went to bed.

Knowing that his mother and father always went to bed an hour after him, he had prolonged all of the things that he had to do so that he wouldn't have to make his way up the dark creepy staircase all by himself. Because at night time, when darkness fell, Kyle was certain that there were always monsters waiting for him upstairs in his room, ready to take him to his doom if he dared to open his eyes whilst lying there within the four corners of his darkened room.

Kyle gripped the duvet tightly as he heard a roar and began to tremble with fright, knowing for sure, that if he opened his eyes now, he wouldn't see daylight.
Once he stopped shaking and the sound came again he realised that it wasn't a monstrous roar at all, but the

sound of his dad shouting up for him to come down and get breakfast.

"It's morning" Kyle said beaming with delight as he slowly opened his eyes and saw beams of daylight pouring through the gaps in the curtains, he was ever so glad it wasn't the silvery glow of the moon that came through the curtains along with the monsters that appeared on his walls at night. Kyle tore the duvet off covering his body, sprang to his feet then made his way over to the door. Just as he was a few inches away from the door Kyle stopped as he saw his baseball cap and coat hanging from the peg. He began to shake as he remembered the monster that stood in its place last night blocking Kyle's exit to freedom and light. Kyle tried to reach for the door handle but his hand wouldn't budge, it just stayed clamped to his side as though weighed down, stuck in sticky mud.

Kyle's eyes widened in fear as the baseball cap and coat began to take the shape of a hideous monster. Kyle began to back away from the door as the monster transformed fully, at ten feet tall and four foot wide the monster blocked Kyle's exit once again. Kyle tried to look away from the monster's hideous face which had slime dripping from its excess skin. He began to back away and as the monster began to inch towards him, Kyle opened his mouth to scream but nothing came out. *It's Daylight, this shouldn't be happening.* Kyle thought to himself. "This must be a dream." He mumbled. "If it isn't, the word daytime will be just as scary as the word bedtime is for me."

As Kyle backed away even further he knocked his leg on the foot of his bed, it really hurt – the pain seared through his whole body. However, he was too frightened to let out a scream, he was transfixed almost in a trance, he kept staring, looking up at the hideous figure edging ever closer towards him. Having nowhere else to go Kyle was forced to sit on the bed and quickly began to crawl backwards. Backing into the wall his mind began to race quickly. *What should I do?* Kyle thought, and then suddenly, Kyle almost smiled as something in his little mind clicked, and as though he was the Master of the Universe, Kyle began to cook up a plan and as quickly as he could. Kyle dived under the duvet and shut his eyes tight, wondering whether he should do it hard or light. As the monster began to roar Kyle hadn't the nerve to worry anymore and pinched his left arm very hard hoping he'd be right in doing so and that when he opened his eyes again if it were daylight he'd be safe.

Kyle's eyes snapped open and he was in his bed, all was quiet and the covers were pulled right over his head. Kyle waited for a second then hearing the birds chirping outside his window, he smiled and sighed with relief. Tearing the covers off from over his head he sat up and saw that it was daylight outside. As he rubbed his eyes and the room came into focus Kyle beamed with joy, knowing that everything was going to be okay.

Kyle got out of bed and made his way across the room and as he got to the door Kyle looked up at his baseball cap and coat and froze once more wondering whether he was still dreaming. Then suddenly the baseball cap and coat began to take form of that hideous shape again. Kyle turned and ran for his bed (with any more speed Kyle would have taken flight) and dived under the cover and waited for a few minutes. After a few long seconds Kyle lowered the duvet and peered out just a little. He looked around the room then focused on the door, seeing that everything looked liked it would in the daylight, he eased the covers off gently this time and made his way over to the door. As he got to the middle of the room he heard a loud roar calling his name and the whole of Kyle's three-foot body began to shake like a leaf in a strong wind.

"Kyle!" The voice roared again, getting nearer and nearer and all Kyle could do was just stand there, rooted to the spot, still shaking. As the voice grew nearer and louder, Kyle shut his eyes and rubbed them, then put his fingers in his ears and wiggled them about just to make sure he was hearing right. After opening his eyes, and taking his fingers out of his ears, he began to walk towards the door again and on doing so he heard the light rap on the door and this time he recognised the voice on the other side of it, the voice belonged to his father.

"Kyle wake up, your breakfast is ready!"

"Coming dad," Kyle called out. He reached for the door handle and opened the bedroom door to see his father standing in front of him. "Good morning son." Mr Mackenzie said with a warm smile looking down at him.

"Morning dad" Kyle replied looking up at his father and returning the smile.

"Come and get your breakfast before it gets cold" his father said and then turned back towards the stairs and descended them slowly.

Kyle leant against his bedroom door and sighed with relief, and thanked the Lord that he was safe and that it was daylight, because for Kyle Mackenzie of Kensingtonville bedtime was the scariest time of all.

Chapter two
The Walk to school

Kyle and his mother stood at their front gate and waved father goodbye, as he set off for his nine to five at the friendly local bank.

"Okay Kyle, fetch your coat, it's time we got you off to school" his mother said, as they turned back towards the house and walked inside.

"Okay sure mum!" Kyle replied and ran up the stairs. As Kyle got to his bedroom, within the timeframe of about 1.5 seconds, he flung open his door tore his coat and baseball cap from the peg, slammed his door and flew down the stairs to the safe area of the hallway.

"Got them!" Kyle said and began putting on his coat as he walked into the living room.

"Good." said Mrs Mackenzie as she walked over to him, kneeling down, she zipped up his coat and fixed his baseball cap so that the peek was in the centre and not at the side.

"Awww, mum!" Kyle groaned

"Kyle you know I don't like you wearing your cap to the side."

"But all my friends do it!"

"So are you saying that if all your friends jumped off a cliff, you would do it too?"

Kyle had a look of deep thought on his face and then began to nod his head.

"Even though you would end up dead when you got to the bottom and would never be able to see me or your father again?" snapped Mrs Mackenzie. Kyle quickly shook his head, changing his mind.

"Well then." Mrs Mackenzie said getting to her feet. "Come on now, let's go." She said, taking Kyle's hand and walking out of the living room, making their way to the front door. As Mrs Mackenzie opened the door Kyle stepped out into the front garden.

"Oh, one minute Kyle." Mrs Mackenzie said as she checked her purse. "I've forgotten my keys inside." she said and then turned back and disappeared into the house to get them.

A few moments later, Kyle jumped in fright as he heard the door bang, turning in alarm he saw his mother standing there with a concerned look on her face.

"Are you alright Kyle?" His mother asked.

"Oh yeah, sure, I'm good!" He lied, as his mother held out her hand for him to take hold of, and Kyle was filled with delight knowing that he was safe. Anyway, he wasn't really scared of the sound of the door, how could he be? He was a man of steel; *I'm ready to take on the bad guys and any other thing that comes my way and tries to mess with me or my world in which I have been chosen to defend!* Kyle thought boldly. Kyle told himself this every day when he was in the company of other people; his "safe zone" as he called it, which was anywhere that he wasn't alone. No one can mess with me, he always declared to himself. Well no one apart from his mother, when she's telling him off she can become very angry, she doesn't have to say anything she just has to give him the evil eye and he'd begin to cry, then she'll stop and he'd save his behind.

But if anyone else tries to cross my path I'll use my super human strength and kick them up their...

"Kyle, you're very quiet today aren't you?" His mother asked breaking his train of thought.

"Just thinking, mum." He replied.

"About what?" His mother asked

"About my super powers and how I beat up the bad guys." Kyle said looking up at his mother who was smiling down at him.

"So who are you today then?"

"The person I am everyday" Kyle replied, screwing up his face and looking at his mother as though she had gone mad to have forgotten who her son was.

"Kyle Mackenzie?" she said grinning.

"Now mummy we both know that, that's just my pretend name." Kyle said very seriously.

"So what's your real name?" Mrs Mackenzie asked playing along.

"Clark Kent of course, silly." Kyle replied.

"If you say so." His mother answered with a smile.

"I do." Kyle replied happily, then silence filled the air whilst Kyle and his mother continued to walk down the street and passed the rows of houses, Mrs Mackenzie paused a few times to say hello to some of the other wives of Kensingtonville along the way as is usual on the school run. As they got to the far end of the road Kyle tightened his grip around his mother's hand hoping he wouldn't see what he normally saw when he reached that certain point. As they reached the last house on the left Kyle heaved a big sigh of relief as he saw that the front porch of the evilest man that had ever ungraced Kensingtonville was empty.

"Thank you God." Kyle whispered to himself and then began skipping a few steps before his mother stopped him.

"Kyle what's wrong with you?" Mrs Mackenzie asked as Kyle skipped too far ahead nearly pulling his mothers arm off in the process.

"Nothing, mum." Kyle said as he stopped and looked back at her.

"So why are you trying to pull my arm off?"

"I wasn't, I'm just so happy that 'Mr Moaning Mean' isn't sitting on his front porch, that I thought I'd have a little skip of joy."

"You leave Mr Spencer alone Kyle, he's just a tired old man that wants an easy life and to be left alone." Mrs Mackenzie replied.

"More like a moaning old man, that has nothing better to do except wait for Corey, Jemel and me to pass, so he can shout at us. You should have heard him the other day…, "You silly little twits, kids should never be born, they do nothing for this world apart from run around and cause trouble. If I had my way I'd get rid of every one of you. Given half the chance I'd blast every one of you into space so I wouldn't have to see your ugly little faces." Kyle said doing his best to imitate the old man's husky voice. "The other day he made Jemel cry, you know". Kyle went on and his mother braced herself for an earful because she knew as well as anyone if Kyle said more than two sentences to you without being asked a question, he could go on forever.

"We were walking along the road and then he just started shouting at us for no reason at all." Kyle said excitedly and his hands became all animated and moved about in the same way that grown ups hands move when they speak. "He stood up on the porch and just started shouting and I can't even tell you some of the words he was saying, 'cause they were rude and Jemel started crying and ran home and before I knew it, he was back here with his dad, and Jemel's dad and Mr Spencer started arguing."

"What did Jemel's dad say?" Mrs Mackenzie asked with interest. "Well we didn't really hear what Mr Richards said, all we heard was Mr Richard's say 'Why Did you make my son cry?' Then we heard Mr Spencer say "Don't you come to me and start shooting your mouth off like you own the place you stupid fool! I know what your type is like; you drive around in your fancy cars and sit in your nice homes with your flash television sets acting like the sun shines out of your backside. Well you know what I say to that? Stick all that fancy stuff where you think the sun shines but doesn't. I hate people like you, and as for your son, he needs a good kick up the backside. If I was down there ten minutes ago I would have given him one." Mr Spencer shouted very angrily and his cheeks went bright red." Kyle said. Then he paused, for dramatic effect and beamed with even more excitement, then carried on.

"Now listen here, you stupid old fool..." Jemel's dad shouted back.

"And that's it?" Kyle's mum asked with a hint of disappointment in her voice as Kyle went silent.

"No, but then Mr Spencer cut Jemel's dad off by calling him a rude word and Jemel's dad really lost his temper and called Mr Spencer a rude word back and then I covered Jemel's ears, Corey covered mine and by that time Corey's brother Reece joined us and was covering Corey's, so none of us heard a thing. But you should have seen it Mum." Kyle said excitedly then went on. "Mr Spencer was shouting at Mr Richards and Mr Richards was shouting back and then Mr Spencer was waving his walking stick in the air and raising his fist."

"Did he step off the porch?" Mrs Mackenzie asked full of excitement.

"No, I don't think I've ever seen Mr Spencer anywhere else other than his porch and church, said Kyle. Oh mum, you should have seen it, it was a sight! Mr Richard's took hold of Jemel's hand and stormed off and Mr Spencer turned and walked back into the house slamming the door behind him."

With all the excitement of Kyle retelling the story of what happened between Mr Spencer and Mr Richards, Kyle forgot about what lay ahead. Because what lay ahead for Kyle was more sinister than Mr Spencer would ever be.

The forest was a place where Kyle would not enter of his own free will. It was a place that cast long creepy shadows upon the ground and where all kinds of horrid creatures crept around. Creatures that were tall, thin, large and small, once inside, Kyle didn't feel like superman at all.

The creepy crawlies of the forest gave Kyle the chills, but his mum always took him this way, as it was the quickest way to school.

As the forest came into sight, Kyle's eyes widened with fear as images flashed through his mind of the creatures that loomed inside, waiting for him behind every tree, to scare him out of his mind.

Once again, Kyle's hand gripped tightly around his mother's as they entered the creepy forest and Kyle fixed his eyes onto the ground because once inside the forest, he knew it wasn't safe to look around. As the sun faded and the shadows grew Kyle knew it was the safest thing to do; however at hearing a sound from not too far away Kyle couldn't help but look up.

"Mummy did you just hear that sound? There maybe a monster lurking around." Kyle asked looking up at his mother and clamping his arm around hers even harder still.

"Don't be silly Kyle, such things don't exist." Mrs Mackenzie replied.

However, Kyle had seen too much evidence and was confused at why she would lie. After all, his life might be on the line and he thought that every parent put their child's life before their own. Didn't they?

"Surely mother you wouldn't want me to die, so why say that monsters don't exist, why tell me that big, fat lie?"

"Because its true Kyle, trust me mother's know best."

As Kyle and his mother walked on, the forest grew darker and creepier still. So dark in fact, it got to the point where Kyle wished he suddenly fell down ill. Anything was better then this, why do grown-ups have to be so lazy? He'd taken the long way before, there was nothing to it really, and it was brighter and far less creepy than this.

A light wind began to blow and Kyle looked up at the trees and saw the leaves as they swayed in the wind. Looking back down on the ground Kyle began to tremble with fright as he saw the shadow of a huge claw hovering over him. There and then he decided he had to take his stand, he couldn't take it any more, he'd had enough and was too scared to be messing around. Letting go of his mother's arm he began to run, and run is what Kyle did, running as fast as his little legs could carry him.

"Kyle!" his mother screamed after him. "What's the matter with you?" Kyle didn't turn back he just kept on running but wasn't so rude as to not reply, he answered whilst he began to run a little bit faster.

"You can walk if you want I don't care, this place gives me the creeps I'm getting out of here!"

"Kyle you stop, right this second and get back here now!" His mother demanded, but Kyle didn't hear what his mother said, his mind was too occupied on getting out of the forest.

Mrs Mackenzie hurried after him and grabbed hold of Kyle's arm. "What's wrong with you Kyle? This place isn't scary; it's all in your mind."

"No it's not." Kyle moaned. "There was a claw back there that was about to grab me so I had to run. I hate this place it gives me the creeps. "

"It's okay Kyle, we're nearly at school." His mother said softly, taking his hand.

"We are?" Kyle asked with glee.

"Yes, just a few minutes more and you'll see the children playing."

As the forest became light again, Kyle and his mother made their exit. Kyle looked up at his mother and calmly said. "Mummy I wasn't really scared, I was playing a trick on you, I mean after all, I am 'Clark Kent the Man of Steel'!"

Chapter three

At School

Kyle liked being at school because once there he had nothing to fear. There were always teachers or other children nearby. Kyle sat at his table doing his maths with his friends, Corey Johnson and Jemel Richards, who sat opposite each other and began to talk.

"My brother has got this movie he's going to let me see." Corey said.

"What's it called?" Jemel asked.

"It's a horror movie!" Corey said grinning excitedly.

"What's it about?" Jemel asked leaning forward with interest.

"Reece said it's about this horrid looking man whose name is Freddy." Corey replied.

"I've heard about that, the man named Freddy wears a sharp claw." Jemel replied.

"That's right!" Corey agreed. "Reece is going to let me watch it do you wanna watch it too?"

"Ah, wicked!" Jemel said happily.

"I know it is." Corey said still grinning with glee.

"So do you wanna?" Corey asked again.

"Of course I do. Can Kyle come too?"

"Who, me?" Kyle said in alarm still thinking about Jemel mentioning the word 'sharp claw', hoping that they didn't see the fear in his eyes.

"Of course I'm talking about you, no one else in here has the name 'Kyle'?" Jemel replied.

"Er…" Was the only sound that could come out of Kyle's mouth and he felt a bit stupid at having nothing else to say.

"You three be quiet!" their teacher, Mr Greenwood, called from the front of the class as he wrote on the chalkboard.

"Sorry Sir." They all said at once then bent their heads as if they where doing their work and as the teacher turned back to the chalkboard Corey let out a little smirk.

"Chicken!" Corey whispered to Kyle, mischievously.

"No I'm not; I can sit through any horror movie."

"Fine, you can come then" Corey said knowing that by calling Kyle a chicken he had won.

"You bet I will, just see if I don't, I'm not a chicken, I'm just as brave as anyone!"

"Fine. Jemel and me will pick you up at five and you'd better come, because if you don't I'll spread the word that you chickened out."

"Fine! I'll be there; you just wait and see, I'll show the both of you that no horror movie can scare me." Kyle put on a good front, not letting them know he was scared. However not having heard all of what the film was about and knowing that his friends would be there, he thought he could handle it.

If Jemel got to finish explaining what the film was about Kyle wouldn't care if they thought he was chicken. He would have just said no, right there on the spot but Jemel didn't, so Kyle wasn't prepared and he got ready to watch a movie about the time he most feared, which included darkness, night-time and going to bed.

As the end of school bell rang, Kyle made a dash for the classroom door and yanked it open. Before Kyle made it into the hallway he stopped in his tracks at the sound of Mr Greenwood's voice calling him to come back. Kyle turned around and walked slowly back to his chair hoping that Mr Greenwood would say 'Class dismissed' before he got anywhere near. However it wasn't to be, so due to Kyle being so hasty, when he got back to his table Mr Greenwood informed the class that Kyle had won them a whole minute of silence. A minute may seem like nothing as a minute goes very quickly. However it was the end of a school day and a weekend at that, when the children could play freely and run about. So like waiting for Christmas morning, or your birthday to come, standing by your desk for a whole minute on a Friday afternoon, the children of Kensingtonville began to think that the sixtieth second would never come.

"Quiet." Mr Greenwood called, and the sixty seconds began. Kyle began to get the strange feeling that he was being watched from behind. As he turned to investigate, he saw lots of hateful eyes glaring at him, for making them all wait another minute and keeping them away from the time they loved most. Kyle turned his head back around real quick and as he did so he saw Corey grinning. Corey loved it when other people got into trouble and his Cheshire cat grin was a silent way of thanking Kyle for allowing him to witness the fact that it was Kyle being told off and not him. For Corey knew when the minute was up Kyle would have to run as though he had fire on his butt. Because keeping a child in Kensingtonville waiting longer than they had to for playtime, was like committing a crime and Corey knew that the other children would make sure Kyle did his time.

Finally the minute was up, "Class dismissed." Mr Greenwood declared and the class filled with noise as the children moved away from their tables and pushed in their chairs. "Have a nice weekend everybody!" Mr Greenwood said as he too stood up and shuffled some papers together making his table look neat.
"Where's Kyle?" Jemel asked looking about and seeing that Kyle was nowhere to be found.
"He must have made a run for it and I don't blame him." Corey said. "When the others get hold of him they'll have his head!"

"Yes you're right, I'm glad it's not me," Jemel agreed shaking his head ever so slowly as they walked across the classroom.

"Poor old Kyle I wish him good luck, if I had a hat on my head I'd take it off for him out of respect just like my dad does when he walks into a room or sees an old lady walking down the street. Even though Kyle was foolish for making a Kensingtonville kid wait any longer than they had to for home time, it was a brave thing to do." Corey said mournfully shaking his head.

"He must be half way across the village by now!" Jemel added looking up at Corey.

"If they haven't got hold of him that is, we may never know." Corey replied.

"Aren't we going to his house to pick him up to watch the movie?" Jemel asked as they left the classroom and made their way down the hall.

"Oh yeah, right, if he's still alive by that time." Corey replied.

Chapter four

The Horror Movie

Not long after Kyle finished his tea, he sat in the living room watching his favourite cartoon, trying to forget about how dumb he was to agree to go and watch the horror movie. Every now and again the thought of going to Corey's house would flash through his mind and every time the scene of him agreeing replayed in his mind he couldn't help but cringe inside and mumble to himself. "How silly was I?" but the last time the scene replayed in his head Kyle had a thought. *Maybe because of the fact that everyone in my class chased me, Corey and Jemel wouldn't come and get me because they'd think I was dead.* Kyle smiled at the thought and hoped they wouldn't come around and when he saw them tomorrow this whole horror movie thing would have been forgotten.

Satisfied Kyle sat back to enjoy the rest of his 'horror-less' show on TV. However, Kyle's thoughts wouldn't come to pass because just as Kyle thought everything in his world was right again, there were two knocks on the front door.

Kyle heard his Mother call his name.

"Yes Mum?" Kyle replied as he got up from his chair and made his way out of the living-room. When he reached the hall he stopped in his tracks at the sight of Corey and Jemel standing in front of him.

"Kyle my best buddy you came out alive, I never thought I'd see you again, Jemel and I thought you were a goner!" Corey said as he and Jemel stepped further into the hallway.

"No man, are you kidding me? As soon as Mr Greenwood called "class dismissed" I legged it! You should have seen me, they were all coming at me, but I was too fast for them, dodging this one and that one, they couldn't even catch me you know, it was like I was Superman!" Kyle said beaming brightly as he lied. Because if truth be told what Kyle did was this: When Mr Greenwood dismissed the class Kyle ran straight for the boys toilets and hid, waited there for five minutes until the corridor was clear then took a different exit out of the building so the other children wouldn't see him.

"What did you do to make the other kids want to chase you?" His mother asked looking down at him firmly and placing her hands on her hips.

"I ran to the classroom door before Mr Greenwood dismissed us." Kyle said in a low voice lowering his head and at the same time hoping that his mother would tell him off and not let him go to Corey's house.

"Well that was quite silly of you, wasn't it?"

"Yes mum." Kyle said turning around and began making his way back toward the living room.

"Kyle, where are you going? Don't you want to go out and play with Jemel and Corey?"

"It's all right mother I know I'm grounded."

"I never said that, you can go out and play."

"Well Kyle was going to come over to my house to watch a movie Mrs Mackenzie."

"Well that's fine by me Corey, as long as he's back by eight."

"Eight it is, Mrs Mackenzie you can count on me, I'll have Kyle back by then, you don't need to worry."

"Well you boys have fun now, and Kyle don't forget your jacket." Mrs Mackenzie said and waved goodbye to the boys then made her way into the living room. Kyle walked over to the coat rack and got his jacket and put it on. Then Corey opened the door and the three of them walked out of the house.

"Wow that was great what you did; did you really dodge the whole class?" Jemel asked.

"Yep." Kyle said smiling broadly as he closed the front door, and they made their way out of the front garden and on to the street.

"Wow that's great!" Jemel said turning to face Kyle and began walking backwards. That means watching this movie should be a piece of cake now. If you're not afraid of all those angry people you shouldn't be afraid of a movie about a man with a claw for a hand."

"I'm not." Kyle said hoping they didn't see the fear on his face.

"So are you ready for this?" Corey said rubbing his hands together excitedly.

"Of course I am! Why wouldn't I be?" Kyle replied.

"Because you look kind of scared." Corey said.

"No I'm not, I'm quite prepared." said Kyle.

"Is that so?" Corey said again with that mischievous grin of his. "My brother said we will all wet ourselves when watching it."

"Well I guess we'll have to wait and see." Kyle said ever so calmly.

**

Kyle sat on the sofa with Corey and Jemel waiting quietly for the film to start. As Reece slipped the video into the machine, the three younger boys all sat back not knowing what they were letting themselves in for, as the movie was about to begin.

Kyle could have sworn that he smelt an unpleasant, but familiar, smell drifting his way. This seemed to be coming from Jemel's direction, whose eyes where already wide with fear as the first scene opened.

As Kyle watched a grimy hand pick up a glove, hammer and a blade and started hammering away at the blade, fear washed over him as a moment later, the man put on the glove to reveal something that looked like a claw and he remembered what he saw in the woods while walking to school that morning as he held his mum's hand tight.

Corey and Jemel jumped back in fright as the man ripped the claw into a sheet and as the claw disappeared and fell out of sight and the screen faded to black and the films title appeared. Kyle could do nothing but just sit frozen in fear. 'A Nightmare' was all he had to read and he knew that putting on the brave front earlier was his dumbest idea.

This film is about bedtime Kyle thought and his mind began to race. *Why did I have to say I wasn't scared? How could I have been so dumb? What on earth have I done?*

All the way through the movie each one kept their cool, or so the others thought. However, by the end of the movie, Jemel's face had turned a pale white, Corey's end of the sofa had permanent nail marks imprinted on it and Kyle sat there as though he had seen a ghost.

"It's time to go now," Corey said as he came to his senses and put back on a brave face. "Oh and sorry Kyle, I can't walk you home; I just remembered my mum said I have to clean my room and I had forgotten all about it until now. Yep, clean my room it's a dirty job but someone has to do it." Corey said, getting to his feet and ushering Kyle and Jemel out of the living room. "What you laughing at" Corey said as he saw his older brother Reece laughing at him.

"You're scared." Reece said.

"No I'm not!" Corey said defensively "You know how mum is when it comes to cleaning my room."

"Sure I do!" Reece replied sarcastically.

"It's true." Corey said annoyed and then pushed Kyle and Jemel out of the living room.

"Well, goodnight both of you, I'll knock for you tomorrow." Corey said opening the door and waiting for them to step out into the darkness.

"See you tomorrow." Jemel said as he stepped out into the garden."

"You said that you were going to walk me home." Kyle pleaded not bothering to hide his fear at having to walk home alone.

"Yeah I did, but you know what mothers' are like when it comes to cleaning up your room and I really don't fancy being grounded on a weekend. Bye." Corey said and then closed the door before Kyle could reply.

  Kyle looked at Jemel and was about to open his mouth and say something, but Jemel cut him off.

"I would walk you home Kyle but to be honest I'm as scared as you are." Kyle nodded understandingly. "I'd have my Dad walk you home, but then he'll want to know why you are afraid to walk home, after all, you do it all the time and if I tell him we watched a horror movie then I'll be grounded and so will you as my father would tell your mother. Sorry." Jemel said sighing with relief at the fact that he only lived two doors away from Corey. Jemel waved Goodbye to Kyle and then walked the two doors down to his house and as Kyle watched him go inside and closed the door Kyle looked up and down the deserted street. There wasn't a soul to be seen and everything was so quiet one could hear a pin drop, the only company Kyle had was the bright yellow glow that was shining down from the street lamp above him.

Kyle turned around and stepped off the pavement and into the road, then stopped as he noticed that if he took three more steps away from where he stood now, he would be in complete darkness.

"Gosh, why did I have to watch that movie and pretend to not be scared?" Kyle said aloud as he stood under the yellow glow of the street lamp.

Get a hold of yourself! A little voice in his head said. *You're really 'Clark Kent the Man of Steel' – remember? You shouldn't be afraid; no harm will come to you.* Hearing the inner voice Kyle felt a rush of energy fill his body and he was once again who he always claimed to be, Superman.

Kyle stepped forward into the darkness not worrying about a thing, he walked down the road as though he was a boy of twelve and not of the eight years that he was. Kyle loved having these secret powers "I bet no other boy of eight could watch a horror movie and then be as brave to walk down a dark and deserted street as I am now." he said aloud with pride. "No they couldn't." He decided.

I bet Corey didn't really have to clean his room, I bet he was just making that up so he didn't have to walk me home and then walk back on his own, Kyle thought to himself then laughed.

"Scaredy cat." Kyle said aloud grinning. A few seconds later the grin faded, together with his thoughts about being Superman, because the street lamp that burnt so bright a moment ago suddenly went out plunging the whole street into total darkness.

"Oh no!" Kyle groaned helplessly as his legs turned to jelly. "Move dumb feet, move!" He pleaded with them as tears welled up in the corners of his eyes.

Kyle just stood there motionless as the tears ran thick and fast down his cheeks, he wasn't even able to lift his hand to wipe the salty wet taste of the tears from his mouth. All he could do was stand there and shake like a three-foot jelly. Kyle was just about to give up all hope and sit on the floor and wail as loud as he could in hope that someone would hear his cries when at that moment Kyle heard a rustle in the bushes from behind him. Jelly legs or not, hearing the rustle in the bushes he began to move and although he thought he wasn't the Man of Steel anymore, at the rate his legs were moving if you had seen him at that point you would have thought he was indeed Superman and if he had fallen over he sure didn't stop to pick himself up only stopping as he reached his front door. Kyle knocked on the door sluggishly as he tried catching his breath back and waited for someone to open it.

Chapter five

Bedtime

Kyle lent against the door trying to catch his breath as he waited for it to be answered, then stumbled into the house and nearly fell to the floor as his Dad pulled the door wide open.

"What on earth is going on here?" Mr Mackenzie asked with concern as he caught hold of Kyle, but Kyle was so scared and out of breath his answer took a while.

"Well?" Mr Mackenzie asked demanding an answer right this minute, but Kyle was deep in thought trying to think of an answer so he wouldn't land himself in trouble.

As Kyle straightened his clothes, buying himself some time, his Dad became impatient, closed the door and headed for the living room and Kyle followed him inside.

"Hi mummy." Kyle said as he entered the living room and sat on the sofa next to her.

"Evening Kyle." Mrs Mackenzie replied looking at her son then as she turned back to the television she did a double take as she saw Kyle's face and notice that it was all sweaty.

"What happened to you?" She asked worriedly.

"Oh nothing mum I just thought I'd run back from Corey's, that's all, it wasn't because I was scared though, I wasn't scared one bit." Kyle said as he sat further back on the sofa.

"What's there to be scared of? Corey only lives at the end of the street." Mr Mackenzie asked meeting his son's eye's and looking at him very suspiciously.

"Nothing." Kyle lied. But his dad knew he was lying and kept his eyes on him.

"Well maybe I was a little scared you see the thing is, the street lamp went out and as I got into the middle of the road I heard something rustling in the bushes so I decided to run down the street. I ran as fast as I could, I didn't even dare to look back to see who it was and took the advice you always give me when you send me to the shop to; be quick and if I fall don't stop to pick myself up."

"Well Kyle", Mrs Mackenzie said looking amused. "You did what any eight-year-old would do. However, there's nothing to be afraid of, it was probably the wind making the bushes sway like that."

"Yes I'm sure you're right mummy, as you know best." Kyle said happily and everything went silent and the family went back to watching the television. However, a moment later Kyle broke the silence and began to speak again, not knowing the trouble he'd be getting himself into. It wasn't his fault, the words just rolled off his tongue and before he could stop himself he had begun. "But it wasn't because we watched the horror movie about this man called Freddy, no it was…" Kyle stopped in mid-sentence realising what he had just done and covered his mouth but he was too late, the damage had already been done.

"What horror movie did you watch?" his father snapped angrily at him and Kyle froze with fear and then looked to his mum for support but she was looking at him with the amount of hurtful disappointment that only a mother could. The disappointed look that his mother gave him was worse than any his father could give. The disappointed look that his mother had on her face there and then was one that could make even the toughest man cry let alone a little boy of eight.

"I'm sorry mummy." Kyle said not being able to take it anymore and burst into tears as he fell to the floor, resting his head on his mothers knee and begging for forgiveness, he explained everything from beginning to end about the discussion that Corey, Jemel and himself had in class and the fact that he pretended to be brave and the real reason why he had made a dash for the classroom door and landed the whole class in a minute of detention and why they all wanted to beat him up.

"Well that was silly to try and act brave when you knew you'd be scared. You should have just told me that you didn't want to go and the reason why and I would have stopped you from going." Mrs Mackenzie said stroking Kyle's hair.

"But I didn't want to look scared and like a baby." Kyle said as he stood up and wiped at his tears.

"So you'd rather punish yourself and sit and watch something you feared, knowing that when it had finished you would not want to go to bed?" His father asked in an annoyed tone.

"Well I didn't want to look the fool father, and be teased by all the other children at school. Because if I didn't go and watch it and word got about that I was a chicken I'd be the laughing stock of the entire school."

"But you are a fool though Kyle, a silly one at that. No one told you to go and follow those two brats. You are grounded for the whole week and when I tell their parents what the three of you got up to your two friends will suffer the same fate. Now get up to bed and I don't want to hear another word from you about this." His father bellowed with authority and Kyle began to shake like a leaf on a tree, on a winter's day.

"B-Bed!" Kyle spat as though tasting a food that he didn't like and wanting to get the horrible taste out of his mouth really quickly.

"Yes, his father added. Now get up stairs and don't give me any of your lip."

Hearing the anger in his father's voice Kyle made it to the living room door ever so quickly. Then turned around and thought he'd give this a try: "Aww, but dad, please can't I sleep down here? You know how much I really hate going up there." Kyle whined.

"Well you should have thought about that before you decided to follow your friends and watch that horror movie."

"But dad you know how much I hate it up there at night." Kyle said helplessly still shaking with fright.

"Yes, I know you do, but it's your own fault, you wouldn't be so scared if you didn't think you had to follow your friends all the time like you always do." Kyle looked from his father to his mother hoping that she had changed her mind and would give him some support. However her look remained the same. Oh how Kyle hated it when she gave him that disappointed look. Feeling defeated and knowing that he had lost the battle Kyle finally turned and walked away from the door. However he reappeared at the door a moment later hoping to give it one more try and win the war.

"I mean, what idiot said that people should have to sleep in the night anyway?" Kyle said putting on a brave and determined face as his parents turned back to the door to face him, then continued speaking. "And that's why I'm going to ask you this, now please don't get mad when I do." Kyle paused and waited for a reaction but when there was none he went on. "I was wondering if I could skip school and sleep while it's light?"

At the look on his dad's face Kyle knew he was beginning to get mad, and suddenly Kyle forgot all about trying to win the bedtime war and as he saw his dad getting up, Kyle turned and ran for the hallway as though he wanted to take flight.

Kyle stopped as he got halfway into the darkened hall and froze not knowing what to do, if he took a step forward he'd be one step closer to his bedroom and Monster City but if he took a step back he'd be closer to his dad, a man who at this moment had no pity and when he got angry Kyle knew he wasn't one to be taken lightly. So taking a deep breath Kyle stepped forward and it took him two steps to reach the other side of the hall, which normally took him ten. Kyle reached the stairs and stuck his hand out in search of the light switch and quickly pressed it but as he clicked it down no light appeared to brighten the stairs.

"Oh no!" Kyle whispered, his voice full of panic, then he flicked it half a dozen times again in disbelief, wishing that it would work and that he could walk calmly up the stairs, but this was not to be and the darkness loomed, so Kyle began to prepare himself for the dash up to his room. Kyle took a few small breaths and rolled up his sleeves, then got in to his sprinting position, ready to run but as he looked up the darkened stairway his legs began to feel numb. Kyle stamped both feet on the step one at a time then began to take the stairs four steps at a time. But no matter how many steps Kyle took, the stair way always seemed to be never ending. "This must be a dream." Kyle said and closed his eyes, which was a big mistake as he missed a step and went tumbling down the stairs. Reaching out for things that would help break his fall, Kyle finally grabbed hold of the banister as he neared the last step.

As something grabbed hold of him he screamed out in fright.

"It's, me Kyle." Kyle heard his mother's soft voice and as he looked up at her she bent down and helped him up and Kyle wrapped his arms around her clinging ever so tightly.

Mrs Mackenzie led Kyle up the stairs and Kyle was ever so relieved knowing she was there. As they got to the top of the stairs and reached Kyle's bedroom Mrs Mackenzie opened the door. Kyle didn't move until she switched on the light. As the room flooded with light Kyle entered and changed into his pajamas, got into bed and happily looked up at his mum. Oh how he loved that beautiful smiling face that beamed back at him, keeping him safe from harm.

"Are you all right?" His mother asked. Kyle returned the smile and nodded taking her arm. "Thank you mummy for bringing me up here, I hate coming up here in the dark."

"You're welcome sweetie, but remember you have nothing to fear there are no monsters in here." His mother said then bent down towards him and kissed him on the forehead. "Goodnight Kyle." She said and Kyle said it back to her and as he watched her walk away he thought he was the safest person on God's green earth. That is of course until he saw the room flood with darkness and heard the closing click of his bedroom door. Because for Kyle Mackenzie of Kensingtonville, bedtime was the scariest time of all.

Coming in 2008

The Creepy Tales from
Kensingtonville

The House on the Haunted Hill